D1134525

PEUK 3462

Published by Ladybird Books Ltd
A Penguin Company
Penguin Books Ltd, 80 Strand, London, WC2R ORL, England
Penguin Books Australia Ltd, Camberwell, Victoria, Australia
Penguin Group (NZ), cnr Airborne and Rosedale Roads,
Albany, Auckland 1310, New Zealand
All rights reserved

ISBN-13: 978-1-84646-025-8
ISBN-10: 1-8464-6025-5

2 4 6 8 10 9 7 5 3 1

Ladybird and the device of a ladybird are trademarks
of Ladybird Books Ltd

Printed in Italy

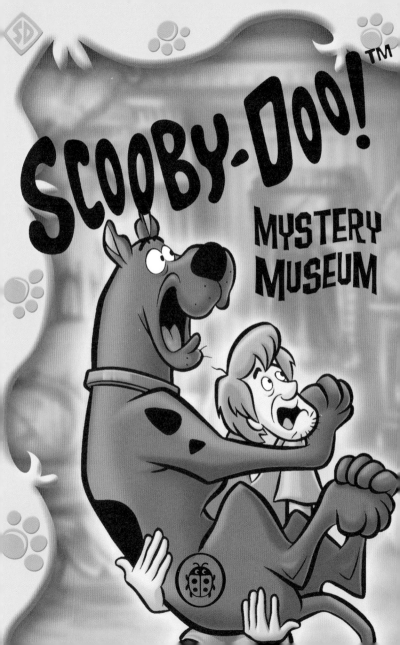

The Mystery Machine squealed to a halt.
Velma jumped out. "We're late!" she cried.
"The Museum of Natural History will close
before we get to see the dinosaurs."
"Scoob and I are sorry, Velma,"
Shaggy said. "But like, we had
to stop for pizza."

"Don't worry, Velma," Daphne said.
"There is time to see the new show."
Fred looked at a map. "The Great Dinosaur
Hall is this way!"
"But the cafeteria is the other way!"
said Shaggy.

Velma led the gang through the jungle room.
Shaggy read a sign. "Gorillas in the wild."
"Ratch out!" Scooby shouted. A gorilla was
swinging right at them!

"Don't worry," said Velma. "These gorillas are puppets. They are wired to move and make noises so we can see how they live in a real jungle." Shaggy sighed.

"Like, I wish those bananas were real."

Next the gang came to the elephants.
The animals raised their trunks.
"Rakes?" asked Scooby.
"Fakes!" said Velma.
"Even those peanuts!" said Shaggy.

Finally, they reached the Dinosaur Hall.
Large dinosaur skeletons peered down at
them. A crowd of people oohed and ahhed.

"Look at that!" Velma said. "A brachiosaur – it looks so real!"

"Jeepers!" said Daphne.

The brachiosaur looked too real. Its great jaws opened and closed. "I am starving," Shaggy said.

"Re too," said Scooby, licking his lips.

Shaggy turned to a security guard.

"Like, where's the best place to chow down?" he asked.

"The cafeteria is this way," the guard said.

He waved his arm, and hit a sign.

"Oops!" said the guard. "I have new glasses. And I still can't see very well. But I can take you to the cafeteria. I have to go that way to start closing the museum."

A few minutes later, Shaggy and Scooby had
emptied the salad bar, the cold drink
machines and everything in between.

All at once, the cafeteria lights flicked.
On, off. On, off.
Shouts echoed all around. Something was
happening!

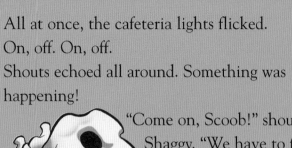

"Come on, Scoob!" shouted
Shaggy. "We have to find
the others!"

They raced back to the Dinosaur Hall. One of the brachiosaur skeletons swung its mighty head. It snapped its jaws. One leg moved, then another. "It's alive!" a boy shouted.

Everyone ran in fright. "Don't panic!" Velma called. A shadow fell over the gang. The dinosaur roared, right over their heads. "Run!" cried Fred.

They raced past the elephants.
The elephants raised their trunks
and stomped their feet.
They sounded angry.

19

Scooby and the gang sped past the gorillas.
The gorillas were swinging from vine to vine.
"Jinkies!" cried Velma. "What is going
on here?"

"It looks like we have a mystery to solve,"
said Fred.
"But it's closing time – let's go," said Shaggy.
"Res! Ret's ro!" Scooby agreed.

"Hmm," said Daphne. "Would you stay for a Scooby Snack?"

"Awhooo!" Howling filled the hall.

"Rikes!" cried Scooby. "A ronster."

"How about two Scooby Snacks?" asked Velma.

"Rokay!"

"Great," said Velma.
"Now, let's split up and look for clues," said Fred. "Daphne, Velma and I will find the security guard. He might know something."

Scooby and Shaggy headed down a long, dark hall. With every footstep they heard strange animal sounds. Then they heard a low, loud moan coming from behind a door. A sign on the door read KEEP OUT.

KEEP OUT

MUSEUM
WORKERS

ONLY

"Zoinks! It's a jungle beast!"
Shaggy yelped.

Shaggy and Scooby raced back
the other way and crashed right
into Velma, Fred and Daphne.

"There's a monster behind that door!
The sign says KEEP OUT. And, like,
that's what I want to do!" Shaggy cried.

"I have an idea," Velma said.
She flung open the door, then
she flipped on the light.

"Thank goodness!" said a voice.

"Hey, it's the security guard," said Shaggy.

"What are you doing here?" The guard waved his arms around the room. The gang saw buttons and levers and switches. "This is the museum control room," he explained.

"I thought so," said Velma. "I bet you stepped inside to close down the museum. But you couldn't see very well."

"I turned off the lights by accident," said the guard. "And when I tried to find the switch, I pressed all the wrong buttons."

With some help from the gang, the guard quickly fixed everything. The museum grew quiet. Then came a long, loud rumbling sound. Everyone jumped. "That's just Scooby's tummy!" said Shaggy. "Hey, can you flip one switch back on? The one for the cafeteria?" "Scooby-Dooby-Doo!" howled Scooby.